OLIVIA™
Takes Ballet

adapted by Cordelia Evans
based on the screenplay by Patricia Resnick
illustrated by Patrick Spaziante

Based on the TV series OLIVIA™ as seen on Nickelodeon™

SIMON SPOTLIGHT
An imprint of Simon & Schuster Children's Publishing Division
New York London Toronto Sydney New Delhi
OLIVIA™ Ian Falconer Ink Unlimited, Inc. and © 2013 Ian Falconer and Classic Media, LLC
For information about special discounts for bulk purchases, please contact Simon & Schuster Special Sales
at 1-866-506-1949 or business@simonandschuster.com
Manufactured in China 0513 LEO First Edition 2 4 6 8 10 9 7 5 3 1
ISBN 978-1-4424-7394-2

Olivia stood on her tiptoes to peek out the window at the driveway.

"I can't wait for Mom to get back with Uncle Garrett!" she said.

"Me neither!" said Ian. "I bet I'm the only one in school with an uncle who plays pro football."

"It's not just about Uncle Garrett," explained Olivia. "Mom is supposed to take me to the ballet tonight!"

Just then the front door opened and in came Mother and
Uncle Garrett.

"Hello, everybody!" said Uncle Garrett. He leaned down
to give Olivia and Ian high fives.

"Hey, I have an idea," he said. "Who wants to go throw
this football around in the front yard?"

"I do! I do!" shouted Olivia and Ian together.

Uncle Garrett showed Olivia and Ian a football play called the Tower of Power.
"Ian, you pass the ball," said Uncle Garrett.
As Ian let the football soar out of his hands, Uncle Garrett lifted Olivia up into the air so she could catch it.
"Touchdown!" shouted Olivia.
"Olivia, it's time to get ready for the ballet," called Mother from inside the house.

At the ballet Olivia squirmed in her seat in excitement.
"It's about to start!" she whispered to Mother as the lights
went down.
A beautiful ballerina wearing a pink tutu came on stage
and began to dance. Olivia wondered what it would be
like to be a ballerina. . . .

Olivia imagined that she was the star ballerina. She and her partner twirled and pirouetted across the stage. For a grand finale her partner lifted up Olivia and threw her into the air.

"Brava!" shouted the audience, tossing red roses at their feet.

Onstage, the real ballerina finished the show and curtsied while the audience clapped. Olivia had a brilliant idea! "Can I take ballet lessons, Mother?" she asked. "Please? I want to be a ballerina!"

"Well, I guess you liked the ballet," said Mother.

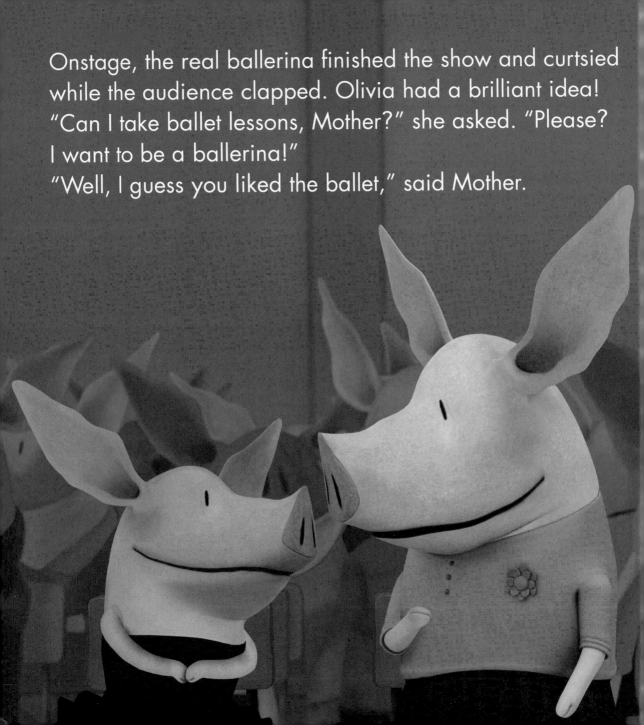

The next day at school Mrs. Hoggenmuller was talking, but Olivia had an important announcement. She raised her hand.

"Yes, Olivia?" said Mrs. Hoggenmuller.

"I'm starting ballet class soon," said Olivia. "So in about two weeks, I'll be able to dance a ballet for Show-and-Tell."

"That's very nice, Olivia," said Mrs. Hoggenmuller.

Olivia's new ballet teacher spoke with a French accent. "*Regardez-moi, leetle* girls," she said. "Look at me!"

"Today we will begin by learning first position," said the teacher. "Please put your feet like this!"
She showed them how to stand with their heels together and their toes pointed outward.

Olivia frowned. Ballet wasn't quite like she had imagined.
She raised her hand.
"Yes?" said the teacher.
"I want to dance with a partner," Olivia declared.
"Ah, a pas de deux," said the teacher. "I'm sorry, but that
is not possible. We have no *leetle* boys in this class."
"Hmm . . . ," said Olivia.

At the dinner table that evening, Uncle Garrett was making everyone laugh with his jokes.

"I have the best little brother in the world!" said Mother.

"No, I do!" said Olivia. "Because Ian is going to come to my ballet class and be my partner."

"Sorry, Olivia," Ian said, shaking his head.

"Fine. Then I'm calling Julian," said Olivia.

"Julian, it's me," Olivia said when her friend answered the phone. "I need you to be my partner at ballet class." "I'm not really a ballet class kind of guy," answered Julian. "Too many people looking at me!"

Olivia turned to Uncle Garrett for help. He took the phone from her.

"Listen, Julian," said Uncle Garrett. "Dance is just like playing football. You might even like it!"

Julian sighed. "One time," he said. "I'll try it one time."

"Yay!" said Olivia.

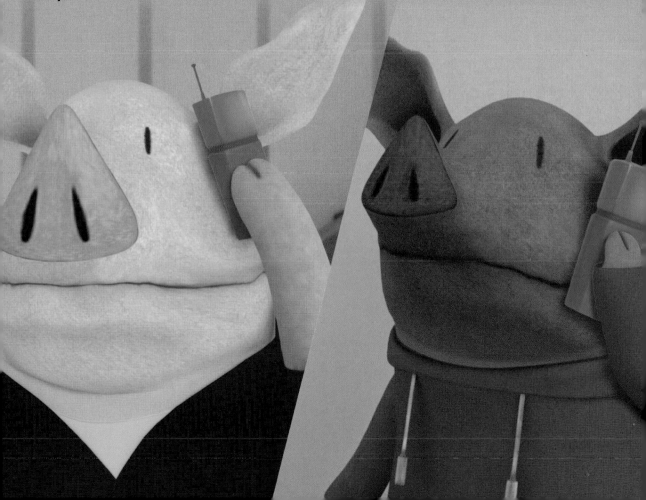

When Olivia arrived at ballet class with Julian in tow, the other girls immediately surrounded him, asking if he wanted to be their partners.

"Julian!" said Olivia. "You're supposed to be *my* partner!"

"*Attendez, leetle* girls—and boy," said the ballet teacher.
"Julian will dance with each girl."
Julian lifted each dancer in turn. Each lift was a little lower
than the last.

"Come on, Julian!" exclaimed Olivia. "We have to practice for Show-and-Tell!"
She twirled and leaped into Julian's arms.

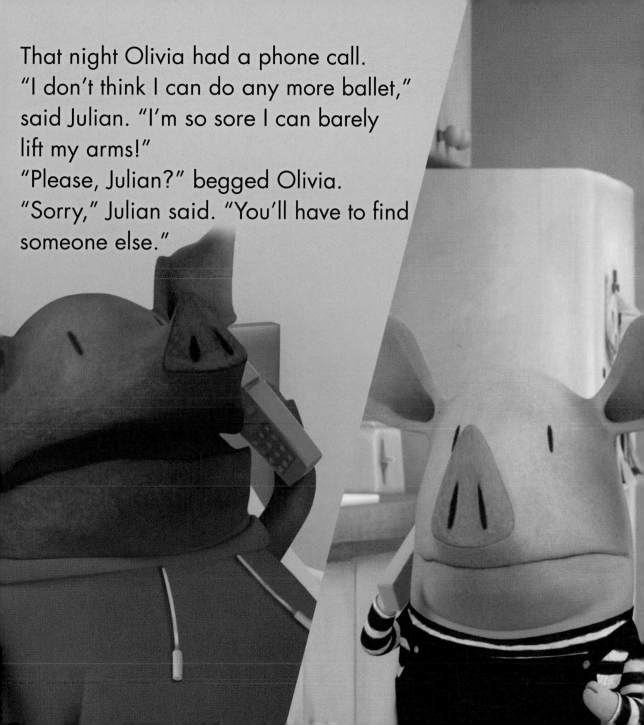

That night Olivia had a phone call.
"I don't think I can do any more ballet,"
said Julian. "I'm so sore I can barely
lift my arms!"
"Please, Julian?" begged Olivia.
"Sorry," Julian said. "You'll have to find
someone else."

Olivia hung up the phone and looked at Ian pleadingly.
"Uh-uh! Never!" he said again.
"I'm sorry, sweetie," said Mother. "I know how much you
were looking forward to this."
"I'd do it with you, but you know I have two left feet," said
Father.

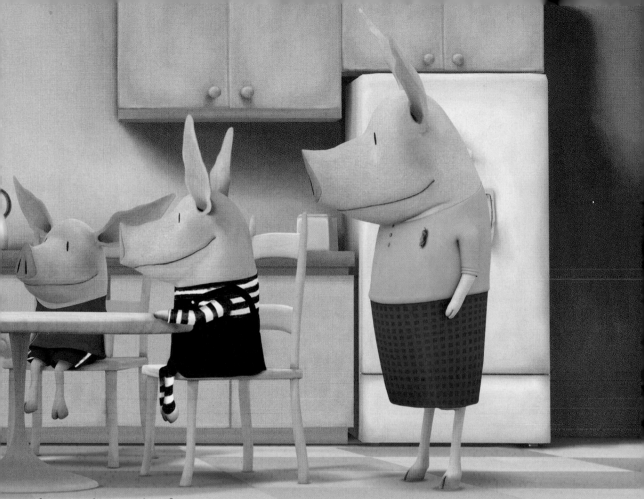

Olivia thought for a moment. "Actually, I know someone who would be the perfect partner . . . graceful, athletic, funny . . . ." She looked over at Uncle Garrett.
"Hey, that sounds like me," Uncle Garrett said, chuckling.
"Oh, wait—I don't know anything about ballet!"
"Don't worry," said Olivia. "I know *tons* about ballet."

Olivia and Uncle Garrett practiced their routine by using
a football to make Uncle Garrett feel more comfortable.
"That's it! Go out for the pass!" said Olivia as Uncle
Garrett pranced backward. "Okay, last move: the Tower
of Power play."
Uncle Garrett lifted Olivia high in the air.
"I think we're ready!" said Olivia.

"Good morning, class. Olivia is going to show and tell us about her uncle," said Mrs. Hoggenmuller the next day. "No," corrected Olivia. "We're going to dance a pas de deux. That's ballet." She turned on her music, and she and Uncle Garrett performed their routine perfectly. When they were finished, the class cheered.

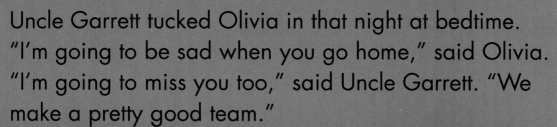

Uncle Garrett tucked Olivia in that night at bedtime.
"I'm going to be sad when you go home," said Olivia.
"I'm going to miss you too," said Uncle Garrett. "We
make a pretty good team."
"On the field and on stage! Good night, Uncle Garrett,"
said Olivia.
"Good night, Olivia," said Uncle Garrett.

THREE   POSITION FOUR   POSITION FIVE

OLIVIA™

Learn ballet with Olivia!

POSITION ONE   POSITION TWO   POSITIO